BIGGER AND BETTER

Kaye Umansky

With illustrations by
Ben Whitehouse

Barrington  Stoke

First published in 2016 in Great Britain by
Barrington Stoke Ltd
18 Walker Street, Edinburgh, EH3 7LP

www.barringtonstoke.co.uk

Text © 2016 Kaye Umansky
Illustrations © 2016 Ben Whitehouse

A CIP catalogue record for this book is available
from the British Library upon request

ISBN: 978-1-78112-558-8

Printed in China by Leo

CONTENTS

For Hannah and Martha

Chapter 1
My First Tiddly

I've always been big. Well, I'm a Giantess. I'm supposed to be.

Everything around me is big. I live in a big castle. I'm married to a big husband with a big name to match – Bigsy. We eat big meals at our big kitchen table. We have a big cat. All our friends and family are big.

With all this bigness around me, you may be surprised to hear that I'm fond of small things. Sea shells. Kittens. Butterflies. I collect thimbles and I keep them on the kitchen windowsill. Small things are my weakness.

That's why I let Jack get away with what he did.

I had never seen a Tiddly in the flesh until the day he turned up on the doorstep. Tiddlies are what we Giants call the little people who live in the land below the clouds.

Tiddly Land. It's a foreign country. I've never been there. Now and then, one of us Giants climbs down via a mountain to throw his weight around a bit and see what's up for grabs. Bigsy's done it a few times. So has Hujo, my brother. But not me. I don't have a head for heights. Or the right clothes. You can't climb down mountains in a cardigan and slippers.

Anyway. I'm rambling. Back to Jack.

It was the cat who spotted him. The milkman had been and I went out to bring in the milk. There was Buster, long and low to the ground with his tail twitching. His eyes were fixed on something behind a carton of cream.

I shooed him away, moved the carton to one side – and there he was. My first ever Tiddly!

"Whoah!" he said, and he flung up a tiny arm to protect himself. "Don't eat me, yeah?"

Eat him? Why would I eat him? He was so … *dinky*! I loved his squeaky little voice and his cute little legs. I loved his baggy shorts. I loved his little cap, which, for some reason, he wore backwards. I loved everything about him.

"I wouldn't dream of it," I said.

He flinched and clapped his hands over his tiny ears. My voice must have sounded like a foghorn to him.

"What are you doing here, little fellow?" I said. In a whisper.

"Climbed up the beanstalk, didn't I?" he squeaked.

"Did you?" I said. "What beanstalk?"

"That big one." He waved an arm. "Back down the road. Grew overnight, didn't it?"

Did it? This was news to me. Mind you, I don't get out much.

"Why go climbing up beanstalks?" I asked. "Don't you like it down in Tiddly Land?"

"Not right now," he said. "My mum's mad at me, ain't she?"

"Is she?"

"Yeah. Just told you that, didn't I?"

Why did he end everything he said with a question?

Mind you, I had plenty of questions of my own.

"Why is she mad?" I asked. "Your mum?"

I couldn't believe anyone could be mad with that sweet little face. Not for long, anyway.

He shrugged. "Sold the cow for magic beans, didn't I?"

"Did you?"

"Yeah," he said. "Then this, like, *massive* beanstalk grew? So I climbed it for a laugh."

"Well, good for you," I said. "Was it fun?"

He looked at me with pity on his face.

"I don't *think* so," he said. "It took, like, for *ever*."

"I bet," I said. "That's a big old climb, for someone your size. What's your name, dearie?"

"Jack, innit?"

'Jack Innit,' I thought. 'Hmm. Unusual.'

"Well, I'm Violet," I said. "Vi for short. Will you come in and have a bite to eat?"

"Sure you won't eat me?" he asked.

"Quite sure!" I said. "The very idea! I'm a vegetarian."

"OK then, cool."

"All right if I pick you up?" I asked.

"OK. Just don't squash me, yeah?"

So I picked Jack up and carried him down the hall and into the kitchen. Buster wound round and round my feet, trying to trip me up. It was clear he had the little fellow marked down as a kitty snack. I shooed him out and shut the door.

With great care, I put Jack down on the table. He hopped up onto the pepper pot, which was just the right size for a seat for him. He took off his little cap and fanned himself. He had lovely hair. Curly.

Now, I can't say my motives were 100% good at this point. The thought had occurred to me that Jack would make a wonderful addition to my collection of little things. I wouldn't trust the cat around him, mind, or Bigsy. I'd have to keep him secret, in a box. Or in my old doll's house, up in the loft. I could take him out every so often, for a private chat. Let him stretch his little legs.

"So," I said. "What's it like, down below? In Tiddly Land?"

"All right," he said.

"Go on," I prompted. "Tell me all about it."

He gave a shrug. "Just a place, innit?"

On second thoughts, the private chats might get boring if that was all he had to say.

"What do you fancy to eat?" I asked. All growing boys are interested in food.

"I dunno," he said. "What you got?"

"I can do you bread and cheese. Or a bacon sandwich." Bigsy loves bacon. I've always got plenty in.

"Bacon, then," he said. "With ketchup."

I put a rasher into the frying pan and cut a slice of bread. I cut off the crusts, and cut it into 4, then 8, then 16. I was having fun, making tiny sandwiches. It reminded me of the tea parties I had for my toys when I was small. Well, smaller.

My little visitor was staring round. "So," he said. "Lived here long?"

"Long enough," I said. "Ever since I married Bigsy."

"Who?"

"Bigsy, my husband."

"What, him?" Jack pointed to the painting on the wall.

In the painting, Bigsy has on his best loin cloth, and he's waving his club in the air and roaring. It was painted by the famous Giant artist Vincent Van Gross, as a prize for Bigsy when he won the Strongest Giant contest by hauling a buffalo over a mountain using only his teeth. He was all muscle then. He's put on a bit of weight since.

He's very hairy, is Bigsy. Van Gross has done a good job of showing all the bits of food and chicken bones caught up in his chest hair.

"That's him," I said, with a little sigh.

"No way is *that* vegetarian," said Jack. "Where's he at now?"

"Down at the Three Ogres for a lunchtime pint," I said. "Don't worry, he'll be ages."

Famous last words. No sooner were they out of my mouth than the floor began to shake and a sound I knew well came to my ears.

It was Bigsy, back from the pub, bellowing his favourite song. Well, the only one he knows all the words to.

"Fee, fi, fo, fum,
I smell the blood of an Englishman!
Be he alive or be he dead,
I'll grind his bones to make my bread!"

"Oh, *man*!" Jack said, and a look of pure horror came on his sweet little face.

Well, Bigsy's singing is terrible.

"Don't panic," I said. "He's back early. I'll put you in the oven. You can hide there until it's safe to leave."

And I picked him up and popped him in. Only just in time.

Chapter 2
I Don't Get It

Bigsy came striding into the kitchen.

"Ooh," he said, sniffing. "Is that bacon I smells, Vi?"

"It is," I said. "I thought I'd do you a sandwich in case you came home early."

"Nice," he said. "But what you doin' to the bread?" He was frowning at the little pile of bread squares.

"It's for the birds," I said. "How was it down at the pub?"

"All right," he said. "Hujo was there. That's why I came back early. Loadsa money, but he never buys his round. He says they'll be payin' us a visit soon."

"Oh," I said. "Really?"

My brother Hujo's married to Bigeeta, my sister-in-law. Their daughter's called Euphonia. I hate it when they visit. They expect a massive tea. Euphonia always plays up and Bigeeta sneers at my thimbles.

"They've gone and bought one o' them new-fangled boxes what keeps the food cold," Bigsy told me. "Begins with a Fuh."

"Fridge," I said, deep in gloom. *Riiiight.* That's why they were coming round. To boast about their new fridge.

We don't have things like fridges in our castle. Bigsy's an old-school Giant – he's not big on modern gadgets. We don't even have a phone. I hinted that I'd like one, and he asked me what was wrong with shouting. I said I'd have to shout pretty loud if I wanted to talk to my friend Mrs Lard, who lives on the other side of Giant Land. We go to Ritzy Bingo together once a month. We like to talk to each other about which cardigan we'll be wearing. It's a big night out.

Bigsy lowered himself into a chair and clapped his hands. I could almost feel Jack flinch from the noise.

"Bring on that bacon sarny, Vi," Bigsy said. "I'm starvin'."

So I made him a huge sandwich. Then I made him five more, because he was still hungry.

"Any big plans for the day, dear?" I asked, when at last he was finished. His beard was full of crumbs, as always.

"Nothin' special," he said. "Might get the swag out. Count the gold bags. See if the hen's layin'. Get the harp to play us a tune."

Bigsy keeps his stolen goods in the cupboard under the sink. All the stuff he's nicked from Tiddly Land over the years. Holiday souvenirs, really. Six teeny-tiny bags of gold, a dinky little hen that lays golden eggs the size of peas and a dear little harp that can play all by itself. I have to say, I like it all. It's all so small, see. But Bigsy doesn't like me to touch any of it, because it's his.

I started on the washing-up while he arranged it all on the table. As always, he counted the gold bags first.

"One," he said. "Two – three – four –"

He always does this. I don't know why. I mean, there are always six. The hen wandered off behind the toast rack to peck at crumbs.

"– five – six," Bigsy finished. "That's all right, then. But the hen's still not layin'."

"Perhaps it doesn't like it in that dark cupboard, poor little thing," I said. "You should let it out more."

"Yeah, but it might fly away," said Bigsy.

I didn't bother telling him yet again that hens don't fly. He's got a brain like a sieve.

"Let's have a bit of music, then," I said.

He poked the tiny harp, and said, "PLAY!" in a commanding voice.

The harp struck up right away with a lovely little tune. It reminded me of 'Bigsleeves' – a song my granny used to play on the organ. I love music. I used to play the piano, years ago.

I picked up the tea towel and hummed along while I dried the dishes. Bigsy spoiled it by trying to sing his 'Fee Fi Fo Fum' song at the same time. He needs to learn a new song. Perhaps I'll write one for him, if I ever get the time.

"I think I'll have a read upstairs," I said.

I like a good read. Right now, I'm reading *Charm and Chubbiness*, about posh Giantesses in long frocks. It's set in the olden days, when Giants had proper manners.

Of course, all this time, poor little Jack was stuck inside the oven. But I knew he would be safe there. Bigsy never goes near the oven. Or the sink. Or the dustpan and brush.

I collected my book, plodded upstairs and lay down on our big bed. Buster settled next to me and started to purr. He had forgotten all about Jack. I opened my book to the right page, but my eyes felt heavy after the first sentence. Well, I'd been up since dawn, slow-roasting a bison.

Several hours later, Buster woke me up by raking my face with his paws, which is how he tells me he wants his supper. In our castle, it's always meal time for somebody. That reminded me that Jack was stuck in the oven without a morsel to eat. I'd not fed the cut-up bread to the birds – perhaps he could have that with a bit of jam on.

In the kitchen, Bigsy was slumped forward in his chair with his head on the table, snoring and drooling in his usual charming way. He's always like that, after he's been to that Three Ogres pub.

But never mind him ... The oven door was open. I rushed across and looked inside. No

Jack. He must have escaped while Bigsy was asleep.

I have to say I was sorry. Not much in the way of interesting conversation, but cute as a box of buttons. Ah, well. That was that.

"Bigsy?" I said. "Wakey-wakey."

"Uh?"

"It's supper time," I said. "Bison and chips. Put your treasure away, now."

"Yeah, all right," he said. "I'm doin' it."

He rubbed his eyes, then picked up the hen between his finger and thumb and returned it to the cupboard, together with the harp. Then he looked around for his six bags of gold.

Which weren't there.

I watched him crawl around on his huge knees under the table. I watched him check behind the salt and pepper pots yet again. I watched him walk over to the fireplace and look up the chimney. Did he suspect Father Christmas?

"I don't get it," he kept saying. "Where are they? I don't get it."

But I got it. Oh yes, I got it all right.

That bad boy Jack. He'd made off with them. Six bags of gold. He'd taken advantage of my hospitality, then robbed my husband. Naughty little tea leaf.

Cute *and* crafty.

Chapter 3
It's a Little Hat

"So, what d'you make o' this beanstalk, then?" Hujo said, with his mouth full of treacle pudding and custard.

It was a week or so later, and the family had made good on their threat and paid us a visit.

I'd spent two days cooking. There was a hog roast to start, followed by mountain pie and mash, a vast cheese board and not one but three puddings.

Bigsy, Hujo and Bigeeta were wading in with a will. Euphonia, of course, was a faddy eater and she wouldn't touch a thing. Right now, her mother explained, all she would eat was cucumber and chocolate buttons, and I didn't have either.

"Beanstalk? You mean that stalky green thing down the road, stickin' up through the clouds?" Bigsy asked, as he chomped on his third helping of trifle.

"Yer, mate, thassit," Hujo said.

"I dunno," said Bigsy. "What do *you* make of it?"

"I don't like it," said Hujo. "Ain't natural."

"I've told Hujo to complain to the council," Bigeeta said, as she helped herself to another slice of my best peanut butter cheesecake. "On. The. Phone."

She likes to rub it in that they've got a phone. She'd already gone on about the fridge for over an hour. The colour – gunmetal silver. The size – extra-big. The number of shelves – 12 with 4 salad trays and an ice tray. The settings – cold, colder and coldest.

I've never seen this wonderful item, but I could give a guided tour.

"Why ring the council?" Bigsy asked, as he poured extra cream onto his trifle.

"To be on the safe side, of course," Bigeeta said. "You never know what might climb up. Besides, it's an eyesore, isn't it? They need to put down weed killer."

"I'm bored," Euphonia whined, and she kicked the table leg. "It's boring, talking about the council."

"All right, darling, we've stopped now," her mother said. "Tell Aunty Vi about the lovely birthday present we got you."

"It's a horse," said Euphonia.

So they had done it, then. They had got her a horse for her birthday. I wouldn't let her loose on a hamster. She's terrible with animals. Buster hates her.

"Who's a lucky girl?" Bigsy cried. "What you callin' this horse of yours, Euphonia?"

"Cloppy," said Euphonia. She sounded bored with it already. Then she added, "Have *you* got me a birthday present, Uncle Bigsy?"

"Er – I dunno," Bigsy said. He leaves everything like that to me. "Have I, Vi?"

"Not yet," I said. "I'm making something, but it's not finished yet."

"As long as it's not another cardigan," Euphonia said. "I don't like cardigans."

I sighed. It was, in fact, another cardigan.

"Did I tell you about my missin' gold?" said Bigsy, who had dripped custard from the trifle all down his front.

"What missing gold?" Bigeeta asked, cutting herself a huge hunk of cheese.

"My six bags of gold went missin'," Bigsy said. "Nodded off at the table, woke up, an' there they was, gone! Looked everywhere. Didn't I, Vi?"

"Six bags!" Hujo gave a little whistle.
"That's a lot o' gold to lose."

"Oh, I don't know," Bigeeta said. "Not *that*
much."

She likes to show off about how much
money they have compared to us. Five years
ago they won the Giant Lottery. Odds of
12 million to 1. Pure luck.

Euphonia had got up and was wandering
around the kitchen. She stooped down in front
of the stove, picked something up and said,
"What's this?"

Oh no! It was only Jack's little cap. It was
down in the grease puddles and egg shells. I'm
not that big on keeping the floor clean.

"It's a little hat," Bigeeta said.

"Hat?" said Bigsy.

"Hat?" said Hujo.

All four of them looked at me.

"Ah! There it is!" I cried. "I was wondering where that was. I'm making new clothes for my doll's house people. Throw it in the bin, Euphonia, it's all greasy. I'll make another one."

"You and your hobbies, sis," Hujo said with a chuckle. "Always had a thing for the small stuff, ain't you?"

"I see she's still got the thimbles." Bigeeta sniffed, without a chuckle. "Grease collectors, I'd call 'em."

I breathed a sigh of relief. I'd got away with it. Mind you, at that point, I had no idea that Jack would be back.

Chapter 4
Can You See the Hen?

A few weeks later, I came into the kitchen to collect my knitting. That cardi for Euphonia still wasn't finished.

Bigsy was out in his shed, doing something secret. He'd been out there a lot the last while, but when I asked him what he was up to, he tapped his nose and said, "Never you mind."

To tell you the truth, I didn't mind at all.

I walked over to the table – and there was Jack, leaning against the toast rack, large as life! Well, in his case, small as life.

"Hey, Vi," he squeaked. "How's it goin'?"

I couldn't believe it. The cheek of him!

"What are you doing here?" I demanded. "I don't know how you've got the nerve to show your face after what you did."

"Yeah, well," he said. "Sorry about that, yeah? It's just all them bags was, like, lyin' around, and I got carried away."

"You mean the *gold* got carried away," I said. "Six bags full. Bigsy's furious."

"But it ain't his, Vi, is it?" said Jack. "He nicked it in the first place, yeah? Human sized, innit? I just stole it back."

He had a point.

"Maybe so," I said. "But I still don't think it's right. Not when I was helping you out. Hiding you and everything."

"Yeah, well, like I said, sorry. Are we cool? You forgive me?"

Of course I forgave him. How could I not forgive that sweet little face? For all his wicked ways, I was smitten all over again.

"You dropped your cap," I said.

"Yeah, well, got a better one, ain't I?"

He pointed to his head. He was indeed wearing a new cap, turned backwards as usual. He had a new outfit of baggy clothes, too.

"You got all that with the gold, I suppose?" I said.

"Yeah," he said. "First thing I did. Went and got myself some new threads. Just as well. Mum spent the rest."

"*Spent it?*" I said. "All of it? What on?"

"Ah, you know," said Jack. "Mansion. Wheels. Clobber. Jewels. Shoes. Handbags. All that. She likes her bling does Mum."

Six bags of gold. Good grief! The woman was shopping mad.

"I hope she put some aside for a rainy day," I said.

"Nah," said Jack. "Not her. She's already had to send some of it back. Bit of a cash-flow problem, yeah? The bank are taking the mansion back. Soon be back where we started."

He gave a little sigh. I felt sorry for him, with such a silly mother.

At that point, the door banged and the floor shook. Bigsy was back from whatever he was up to in the shed.

"Vi?" he shouted. "Where are you? I've hurt meself."

"Oops," said Jack. "Here we go again. Don't worry, I know the way."

He shinned down the table leg, sprinted across to the oven and climbed in, just in time.

Bigsy came into the kitchen holding up his thumb, which was bleeding.

"The chisel slipped," he said.

"Stick it under the tap," I told him.

"Ow," he moaned, as the water flowed over his thumb. "Ow, ow, ow!"

He can be a right wuss sometimes.

"Sit down and rest," I said. "I'll do you some sausages."

He slumped into a chair and watched me put 20 sausages into the frying pan. Sausages always cheer him up.

A short time later, he was tucking in to his meal. Grease ran down his chin, and he was making horrible slurping noises.

"I'm just popping out to the garden," I said. "See if the washing's dry."

It was a nice, sunny day outside. I took the clothes down off the line and threw them in the basket. Then I lay down in the hammock Bigsy had rigged up for me and kicked off my slippers. Buster jumped on my lap. Before I knew it, I'd dozed off.

I was woken by a terrible roar from the kitchen.

Yet again, Bigsy was on his hands and knees with his massive bottom in the air, crawling around in the dirt. I still hadn't got round to sweeping up.

"What in clouds are you doing, Bigsy?" I asked.

"The hen!" he bellowed. "I've lost the hen!"

"Isn't it in the cupboard?"

"If it was in the cupboard it wouldn't be lost, would it?"

He had a point. "Why did you take it out?" I asked.

"Wanted to see if it'd lay, didn't I?" he said. "I just closed my eyes for a minute cos I felt a bit woozy with me thumb. Oh, where's it gone, Vi? D'you think it's flown away?"

No. I didn't. The oven door was wide open –
and there was no sign of Jack.

Oooh! The little rascal!

Chapter 5
I Want a Camel

"So the hen flew away?" Hujo asked. "That's bad luck, that is, mate."

We were sitting around the table in my brother's castle. They don't invite us that often. I can't say I mind. They make you take your shoes off the minute you arrive. They don't even offer you a cup of tea. Too keen to give you a guided tour of their latest purchases. The new sofa. The footbath. The exercise bike (which I swear nobody uses). All the white goods in the kitchen, including the massive great fridge.

You have to go "ooh" and "ahh" and pretend to be interested. It's very tiring.

Bigeeta doesn't cook. They always send out for Chinese takeaway. It comes in huge foil trays and you eat it with sticks, which I can never get the hang of. And they always forget I'm veggie, so all I can eat is the rice. Bigsy ignores the sticks and uses his hands.

Euphonia doesn't do Chinese takeaway. Her mother said she was eating nothing but raisins and beetroot at the moment. I had given her the cardigan I'd knitted for her birthday, and she hardly looked at it. Even though I'd added horseshoe buttons. Cloppy, the birthday horse, was twiddling its hooves in the garden outside, looking fed up and a bit unloved.

"Mind you, that hen had stopped layin' eggs," Bigsy said. "Dunno why."

"The council's still done nothing about that beanstalk," Bigeeta said. I could see she was keen to move on from hen talk. "I don't know why we pay our taxes."

"We don't pay taxes," Hujo said, as he speared the last crispy duck pancake.

"Still," said Bigeeta. "Taxes or not. They should do something."

"Still got that little harp, have you?" Hujo asked Bigsy. "The one what plays all by itself?"

"Yep," Bigsy said. "It'd break my heart if that went missin'. We likes a bit o' music, don't we, Vi?"

"We do," I said.

I tried picking up some rice with the silly sticks, but it dropped all over my dress. It was my best dress, too. The one I wear on the rare times I go visiting.

"Oops-a-sunflower," said Bigeeta. (We're Giants. We only do big flowers. Daisies are too small and sissy.) She handed me a napkin. "Here, Vi, wipe yourself down. Good job it's an old frock."

Bigeeta has a lot of dresses. Huge things, like tents with flowers on. She buys lots of jewellery too – jangly earrings and glittery bangles. She'd probably get on well with Jack's mum. She dresses Euphonia in pink frills, which don't suit her. The pair of them are always out shopping, or ordering tiaras online. Well, they have a lot of time on their hands. No chores to do, see. They pay a cleaning firm to come in every Monday and Friday. It's all right for some.

"I'm thinkin' I might climb down to Tiddly Land," Bigsy said. "Get meself a few bags o' gold. Replace the ones what got stolen."

Really? This was the first I'd heard of it. It was a terrible idea. Bigsy's no spring chicken.

Too old to be climbing down mountains, that's for sure. I would have a word with him about that.

"Yeah?" Hujo said. "I might join you, mate. Years since I been down there."

"You'll do no such thing, Hujo!" Bigeeta snapped. "I'm not having you go back to the bad old ways! It's not as if we need the money."

"Yeah, yeah, all right," said Hujo. "Keep your hair on."

"I'm bored," Euphonia announced, for a change.

"Eat your beetroot, darling," her mother said. "I got it in special."

"Beetroot, yuk," said Euphonia, and she pulled a face. "It's disgusting and I won't eat it any more. I only like papaya and pumpkin granola now."

"What's that when it's at 'ome?" Bigsy asked. He's a meat man. Fancy cereal is a long way outside his comfort zone.

"We don't have any granola, angel," Bigeeta said. "Just finish up your raisins, there's a good girl."

"I don't like raisins any more either. They look like rabbit poo."

Hujo and Bigeeta looked at each other and sighed. They didn't even tell her off for using bad language at the table. If she was my daughter, there'd be trouble.

"How's the ridin' comin' along, Euphonia?" Bigsy asked, as he scraped out the last of the chop suey.

Euphonia shrugged and made a face.

"She's not tried it yet," Bigeeta said.

"Why's that, then?" Bigsy asked.

"I don't want a horse any more," said Euphonia. "Horses are *boring*. I want a camel."

I kid you not. That girl was more than I could take.

"We should be going, Bigsy," I said, and as I stood up, I sent rice showering everywhere. "Time's getting on."

So we went home, back to our own castle, which was smaller, shabbier and poorer in every way. While we were gone, there had been a small fire in the kitchen, because I'd left the gas on.

It was a horrible ending to a horrible day.

Chapter 6
Save Me!

You might not believe that Jack would come back a third time to rob us.

But he did, the cheeky wee blinder.

A couple of weeks later, we had eaten supper and were in the kitchen, listening to the radio. Well, I was.

The radio is the nearest thing to a modern gadget we own. Bigsy picked it up from a jumble sale. It's crackly, but you can just about hear it.

There was a nice concert of Giant music on. All the jolly old songs I like best. 'He'll Be Kicking Down The Mountain When He Comes.' And 'All The Nice Girls Love An Ogre.'

I was sitting in the rocking chair and humming along with my eyes closed. Bigsy, as usual, was snoozing and drooling. He had joined in with 'Fee Fi Fo Fum', but once that was over, he lost interest.

If it wasn't for the cat, I would never have noticed what was happening under our very noses. He was sprawled in my lap, purring away – then I felt him stiffen. A low growl came from his throat.

I opened my eyes – and blow me if it wasn't that little scallywag Jack again! The door of Bigsy's swag cupboard was wide open – and

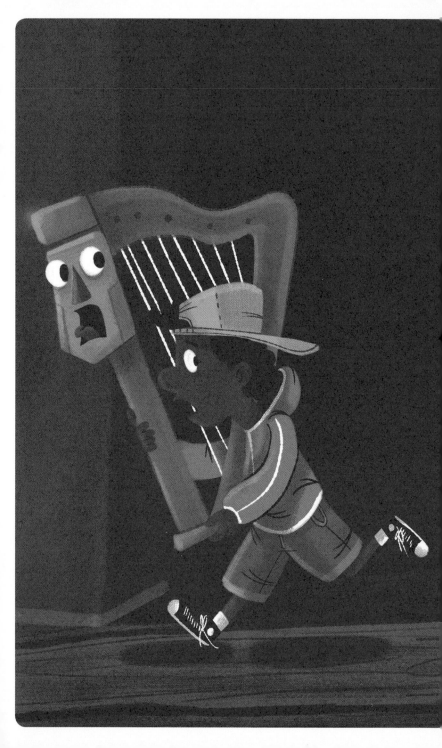

there he was, running at top speed for the kitchen door. In his arms was the golden harp!

I opened my mouth to shout a warning – but for some reason, nothing came out. There was something about those little legs. I know it's daft, but I just couldn't let him get hurt. Bigsy would step on him like a snail in the garden, I knew that.

But the harp had other ideas. "Save me!" it cried, in its silvery voice. "Master! Oh master! Save me!"

"Uh?" said Bigsy. He struggled out of his chair and his eyes fell on Jack, who was nearly out the door. "What the – oi! You! Come back 'ere, you good-for-nothin' little wretch!"

He took a giant step forward. At the same time, Buster leaped off my lap as if he'd been scalded. Bigsy tripped over him and came crashing down on his knees, squashing the poor cat with his belly. He grabbed at a chair to help him pull himself up. The chair fell over on both of them. Buster screeched and lashed out, and Bigsy got a nasty scratch on his nose.

"Ow!" Bigsy shouted. "Me knees! Me 'ead! Me nose! Where is he?"

While all this was happening Jack was making his getaway. For a little chap, he could certainly go. I could hear the harp still calling out "Save me!" but, by the sound of it, Jack was already a good way down the hall.

"Forget it, Bigsy," I cried. "He's not worth it!"

"Not worth it?" he bellowed, as he heaved himself to his feet. "He's nickin' my *harp*, the thievin' little toe rag!"

Buster had taken himself off to a corner and was licking his rumpled fur. He had a snooty tilt to his head as he pretended that nothing had happened. He had moved on.

Not so Bigsy. His temper was up. He gave a great roar, as he crashed from the kitchen and pounded down the hall to the front door. I knew it would be open. There's something wrong with the lock and it won't close all the way. I keep asking him to fix it, but he's been too busy with his secret shed project.

"Bigsy!" I shouted. "Don't you go trying to climb down that beanstalk! You'll come a cropper!"

No reply. Just distant roaring and clomping.

I hurried out of the castle and gazed along the road. There was nothing to see but a huge dust cloud in the distance.

Well, what was I to do? I only had my slippers on.

I went back to the kitchen and gave Buster his supper. Then I made myself a cup of tea, got a plate of fig rolls to dunk in it, and sat down in peace with the crossword puzzle. Bigsy'd be back soon, wouldn't he? He wouldn't be daft enough to attempt a climb down the beanstalk. Not at his age and weight. Would he?

I waited up all night. I finished the fig rolls and the crossword. There was no sign of him.

The next morning, Hujo came over. I guessed there was something wrong, because Bigeeta and Euphonia weren't with him. He must have got them to stay at home, because he had bad news and he thought it'd be better to break it to me on his own.

The beanstalk was no more, he told me. Nothing to do with the council. It seems Bigsy was on his way down when some nasty little Tiddly got an axe and chopped right through it. The beanstalk fell and so did my poor, silly, massive husband. He hurtled down to certain death.

Oh. I wasn't expecting that.

Chapter 7
My Business Brain

I was terribly upset, of course, and did a lot of weeping those first few days. Well, we'd been married for years. I forget how many. I got out the wedding photo album. There we were, all young and hopeful and looking forward to the future together. Neither of us was quite so big then.

I felt even worse when I found what Bigsy had been doing in the shed. He'd been trying to make a special display cabinet to show off my thimbles. It was a bit wonky – the shelves were on a slant, and the glass was splattered with blood where he'd cut his thumb with the chisel.

When I carried the cabinet back to the kitchen, both its doors fell off. Never mind.

But you can't sit around moping for ever. Life goes on. There's cardis to be knitted and bingo to be won. At least I didn't have any money worries. I haven't told you this bit yet, so I'll explain.

The hen, you see, hadn't stopped laying at all. For years, I had been collecting her golden eggs. I'm not like Jack's mother – I believe you should put something aside for a rainy day. I had hundreds of those eggs. I kept them in little glass jars in my old doll's house. They looked ever so pretty, but more to the point I intended to surprise Bigsy with them when we were old and grey and in need of a pension.

My friend Mrs Lard came over to pay her respects. I confessed about the golden eggs over tea and a plate of homemade coconut castles.

"Am I awful?" I asked her. "After all, it was his hen."

"Of course not, Vi," she said. "You were just being business-like. If I was you, I'd go on a little spending spree. Cheer yourself up. I'll come."

And that's just what we did. We went out and I bought myself a trouser suit in cheerful yellow. I've never worn trousers. Bigsy didn't like me in them. I got a couple of dresses too, and a pair of shoes with gold chains and kitten heels. I had my hair done. I threw out all my tatty old cardigans and replaced them with a selection of colourful shawls. The girl in the shop told me they have something called a "boho vibe". I bought a pair of glittery earrings. I could have given Jack's mum a run for her money. Mrs Lard bought a new raincoat. I paid for it, but in return, she treated me to fancy coffee in Bigbucks, the expensive new place in town. It was nothing but froth. I wish I'd ordered tea.

I got in a team of painters to spruce up
the castle. I ordered a fridge and a washing
machine. I had a phone put in, so I could ring
Mrs Lard whenever I felt like a chat. I bought
Buster a little bell for his collar, but I drew the
line at a cat bow-tie in tartan.

Bigeeta and Euphonia came round to visit.
Bigeeta didn't seem all that pleased when she
saw the improvements to both me and the
castle. She just sniffed and said, "About time."
Euphonia didn't say anything, only asked if I
had any tofu or guava fruit. I didn't. I didn't
have any tahini either, or mung beans, jelly
babies, sorrel root or organic flaming oatcakes.

They didn't stay long, because they were off
to look at camels.

I was lonely without my Bigsy, of course.
Most nights I stayed home and read or looked
out the window, stroking the cat and listening
to the hum of the new fridge. Sometimes, I
rearranged my thimbles.

Then – one night before bed, when I was in the kitchen making a mug of cocoa – the impossible happened!

The front door banged. The floor shook. And I heard a familiar voice boom out.

"Vi? You there?"

My heart missed a beat. The mug dropped from my hand.

"Bigsy?" I asked, and my voice wobbled. "Bigsy, is that you?"

It was!

He came limping into the room and I ran into his lovely big arms.

He hadn't died after all! Oh, he'd had a nasty fall, of course. It knocked him out cold. That wicked little Jack had left him for dead. But it takes a lot to kill a Giant.

When Bigsy had come round at last, he'd made for some distant mountains. All the way he had to hide in forests and duck behind hills to avoid any more meetings with Tiddlies. He lived on wild berries and mushrooms and a rabbit now and then. It had taken him weeks, but one day he reached those distant mountains and somehow managed to drag himself up one, then up past the clouds and back into Giant Land.

As you can imagine, he was in a shocking state. He was scratched, bruised and filthy, his hair was matted, he had a big lump on his head, and his poor sore feet were all blisters. He'd lost a lot of weight, too, but that was no bad thing. But he's tough, is Bigsy. With a bit of my best TLC, he recovered in no time.

To my surprise, he liked my new look. Even the yellow trouser suit. He liked my hair. He liked what I'd done with the castle, too. Well, it does look nice. He liked the fridge best, because it means we can buy frozen bison burgers in bulk.

I had to confess about the golden eggs, of course. But he was fine about that. I think he was impressed by my business brain.

I don't know what happened to Jack. I don't know if he's still got the hen or the harp. I don't care, anyway. I've gone off him. I don't know if all Tiddlies are like him. Sneaky and mean and ungrateful. I hope not.

Bigsy's changed quite a bit, since the accident. He spends all his time at home, with me. He doesn't go to the Three Ogres or sing the 'Fee Fi Fo Fum' song any more. I've written him a new one, in fact. He's still learning the words.

Last night, when we were drinking our cocoa together, he said something really sweet. He told me he'd only made it home because he wanted to get back to me and my bacon sandwiches.

That's my boy. Big in body, big in appetite, and big in heart. Big in every way. And big is, of course, better. At least, in my book it is.

I'll have to stop now, because we're off out to dinner. There's a new place opened that does two Giant meals for the price of one every Tuesday. I'm wearing one of my new frocks and Bigsy's wearing a suit, for once. He's shaved his beard off, too.

I shouldn't say it myself, but he really does look quite handsome.

Oh – one more thing. You might like to hear the new song I wrote for Bigsy – to replace 'Fee Fi Fo Fum'. He's having trouble learning it, because there are more than four words. But he'll get there in the end. So, here it is. Hope you like it.

Vi's Song

Tiny feet are kind of sweet
But big feet are better!
Little knees are nice to squeeze
But big knees are better!
Small is cute, I don't dispute,
But when my Bigsy's in his suit
There's nobody I'd substitute
Cos big is better!

Big is better!
Buy that outsize sweater!
Sing it loud and sing it proud,
Big Is Better!

Our books are tested
for children and young people by
children and young people.

Thanks to everyone who consulted on
a manuscript for their time and effort in
helping us to make our books better
for our readers.

KAYE UMANSKY has written lots of laugh-out-loud "fractured fairy tales", including ...

This is The Frog Prince as you've never read it before.

This is Sleeping Beauty as you've never read it before.

This is Cinderella as you've never read it before.

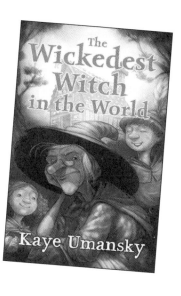

This is Hansel and Gretel as you've never read it before.

This is Snow White as you've never read it before.